A CARTOON NETWORK ORIGINAL

VOLUME

BOOM! Studios, 5670 Wilshire Boulevard, Suite 400, Los Angeles, CA 90036-5679. Printed in China. First Printing.

ISBN: 978-1-68415-133-2, eISBN: 978-1-61398-872-5

RINK!

ADVENTURE TIME™
Created by **PENDLETON WARD**

"THE FORGOTTEN PRINCESS"
Written by
PHILLIP KENNEDY JOHNSON
Illustrated by
ANTONIO SANDOVAL
Letters by
JIM CAMPBELL

"BODY BY JAKE"
Written by
MAX DAVISON
Illustrated by
LUCA CLARETTI
Colors by
ELEONORA BRUNI
Letters by
TAYLOR ESPOSITO

"MAGIC MAN & TINY MANTICORE"
Written by
JAI NITZ
Illustrated by
DEVMALYA PRAMANIK
Colors by
TRIONA FARRELL
Letters by
ADITYA BIDIKAR

"CHOCK FULL O' STUFF"
Written & Illustrated by
DAVID DEGRAND

"FINN VERSUS FINN"
Written by
JUSTIN JORDAN
Illustrated by
MATTIA DI MEO
Colors by
JOANA LAFUENTE
Letters by
JIM CAMPBELL

"P-B-M-O"
Written by
CRYSTAL SKILLMAN &
FRED VAN LENTE
Illustrated by
DANIELE DI NICUOLO
Colors by
WALTER BAIAMONTE

"FOR THE LOVE OF OOO"
Written & Illustrated by
E JACKSON

"WHERE THE SLIME LIVE"
Written & Illustrated by
STEVE SEELEY
Letters by
JIM CAMPBELL

"B-MAX"
Written & Illustrated by
ANOOSHA SYED

"THE THUMB-DERDOME"
Written & Illustrated by
MARIE ENGER

"CRAB ATTACK"
Written & Illustrated by
JENNA AYOUB

"MIGHTIER THAN THE FIST"
Written & Illustrated by
BEN PASSMORE

"BROKEN"
Written & Illustrated by
BETHANY SELLERS
Colors by
JOANA LAFUENTE
Letters by
JIM CAMPBELL

"THE BUMMER STORY OF CHOOSE GOOSE"
Written by
LEAH WILLIAMS
Illustrated by
RYAN JAMPOLE
Colors by
JOANA LAFUENTE
Letters by
JIM CAMPBELL

"COSMO CUSTODIAN"
Written & Illustrated by
IAN HERRING

"BANANA TRAINING VIDEO"
Written & Illustrated by
KINOKO EVANS

Cover by
PAUL POPE

Designer
HELSEA ROBERTS

Assistant Editor
KATALINA HOLLAND

Associate Editor
MATTHEW LEVINE

Editor
WHITNEY LEOPARD

With Special Thanks to Marisa Marionakis, Janet No, Curtis Lelash, Conrad Montgomery, Kelly Crews, Scott Malchus, Adam Muto and the wonderful folks at Cartoon Network.

SKREEEEEEEEEBLE

WAA AAAUU GGUBAG UHBAGU HBAG UH!

BAHAHAHAHA! THAT WAS A GOOD ONE, MAN, I GOT YOU GOOD!
DANK THAT NOISE! I WAS READY FOR YOU.
YOUR TURN! GO FIND YOU A GOOD HIDING SPOT.

COUNT TO FIFTY THIS TIME!
WHIK WHIK WHIK WHIK
ONE... TWO... THREE...

OH MY GLOB! A TOOTHY UMBRELLA BABY!
WHIK WHIK WHIK WHIK WHIK WHIK
THESE THINGS ARE SUPPOSED TO GRANT WISHES!

FORGOTTEN PRINCESS

Written by Phillip KENNEDY JOHNSON
Illustrated by Antonio SANDOVAL
Lettered by Jim CAMPBELL

BUMP
WHEN JAKE COMES CLOSE, I'LL BE ALL LIKE,
WAOOOWWWWW!
AND THEN HE'LL BE LIKE,
GAH-OOOOOOK!
I DON'T KNOW ABOUT THIS "FORGOTTEN" BIZ, BUT WHATEVS.
Oh, THIS IS GONNA BE WICKED HARDCORE.
Huh! THAT LOOKS LIKE SOME PRIME REAL ESTEEZ.
FOR THE FORGOTTEN, ONLY IN.
WHOA.
FOR THE FORGOTTEN, NO OUT.

Kinda stinks in here.
Like butt-shrooms, or something.
MAN, IT'S HARD TO BREATH IN HERE. THINK I BETTER FIND A NEW--
UUURGH!
C'MON, C'MON!
creaak
AW, NO!
CAN'T GET OUT THE OTHER WAY, SO I'LL GO THIS WAY.
BOOMP BOOMP BOOMP BOOMP
SOMEBODY LEMME OUT! JAAAAKE!
FORGOTTEN
AND THEN I'L FIND SOM OTHER--
WAOOOWWWWW! WHO'S IN HERE?!
WHAT THE FLIP-FLOP, MAN, HOW DO I GET OUT OF HERE?!
FORGOTTEN

VOOSH
FOOM
FTOOM
WHAT THE BJORKZ!
HELP!
SOMEBODY HELP US!
STOP
SMASH
BOOM, SUCKA!

WHAT'S WITH ALL THE BONE-BAGS JACKIN' UP THE PLACE?
IT'S THE ARMY OF THE *FEATHERY GOAT MAN!*
NOT NOW, KENNY! CAN'T YOU FEEL HOW HOT THE WIND IS GETTING? HE'S COMING!
FEATHERY-WHAT NOW? WHAT IS THIS PLACE?

THIS IS THE KINGDOM OF *FORGOTTEN* STUFF! EVERYTHING FORGOTTEN COMES HERE!
QUICK, THERE'S SHELTER UP AHEAD!

SLAM
I THINK HE SAW US! BE READY TO RUN OUT THE BACK!
OH MY GOSH...YOU'RE *NEW,* AREN'T YOU?!
IS THERE ANYONE ON THE OTHER SIDE WHO MIGHT REMEMBER YOU?

IF YOU GET PULLED BACK, *YOU HAVE TO REMEMBER US!* WE CAN'T GET OUT IF YOU DON'T!
KRAK
IT'S *HIM!* C'MON, OUT THE BACK!

ROARR
THE FEATHERY GOAT MAN'S COMING! PLEASE, GET US OUT!
KENNY, NEW GUY, *COME ON!*
YOU GO! NO FEATHER-GOAT DINGUS IS GETTIN' UP IN OUR BIZ!

KARAAAGH

HEYAAAA--

WAOOOWWWWW!
SMASH
GAH-OOOOOOK!

HAHAHA! THAT WAS A REALLY GOOD ONE!
Oh, MAN! MAN, I JUST...
WHERE'D YOU GO, JAKE?

Oh BRO, IT WAS BA-NOWOW! I SAW A TOOTHY UMBRELLA BABY! I CHASED IT ALL OVER, BUT THOSE THINGS ARE KILLER-DILLER FAST!
YEAH, BUT YOU DIDN'T, LIKE...FORGET ABOUT ME, DID YOU?

WHAT?! C'MON, HOMIE, I COULDN'T FORGET YOU! WE'RE LIKE PEANUT BUTTER AND JAY-JAY!
YOU OKAY? YOU SEEM KINDA, I-DON'T-KNOW, OR SOMETHIN'.

YEAH... YEAH, I'M OKAY. MUST'VE FALLEN ASLEEP IN THERE.
Oh, WEIRD. YOU HAVE A BAD DREAM?

Um...I GUESS SO.
I DON'T REALLY REMEMBER.
THE END

The Candyhoga river is overflowing! For some reason, there's all this *extra water* coming from the *Ice King's castle.*
If this keeps up, the whole Candy Kingdom could flood! You gotta help us!
Well, Jake, a seemingly unsolvable challenge like this calls for something special.
Way *ahead* of you, *buddy!*
The Jakesuit
BODY by JAKE
WORDS MAX DAVISON
ART LUCA CLARETTI
COLORS ELEONORA BRUNI
LETTERS TAYLOR ESPOSITO

How you gonna use the Jake Suit this time, Finn?
HEFT
We have to stop that old river from flowing. So what's the best way of doing that?
By turning it into *a new lake!*

And now to break it in with the *world's biggest cannonball!*
KA-SPLASH

Why thank you, Super-Strong Finn!
All in a day's work for a strong hero like me.
Finn the Human: the *strongest* there *is!*
Uh, buddy? Don't forget the *"Jake"* part of the *"Jake Suit."*

You couldn't have lifted that boulder without me, so I don't want you taking *all* the credit!
And you've been doin' that *a lot* lately!
I mean, it does help just *a little bit...*

But it's my brains that come up with how we lift.
And it's my brawn that's actually carrying all that stuff!

SNAP
Well, there's only one way to conclusively find out who's stronger...

A weightlifting competition!
YEAAAH! Feel the burn!
Oh it is so on! I am pumped!

KRAK
Here's how it works. We each point to something and the other person has to lift it up. Deal?
Deal!

So how about you try and lift that tractor?
Challenge accepted!
And remember to lift with your legs! I don't want you hurting your back.

Heh heh. No way he'll be able to lift something that heavy!
Soon there'll be no doubt that I'm the--

Strongest?! WHA-HUH? How'd you do that?!
Easy...

"...There was a nearby geyser!"
MIND OVER MATTER

My turn. How about you lift...the Tree Fort!
No prob! And since we live there, I'll even be extra careful not to move any of my stuff.

Gonna lift it so high that you might have to crane your neck a bit to see it!
CREEEEK

Ta-da! Everything all right in there, BMO?
We're good, Macho Strong Jake! My bed only shifted two centimeters!

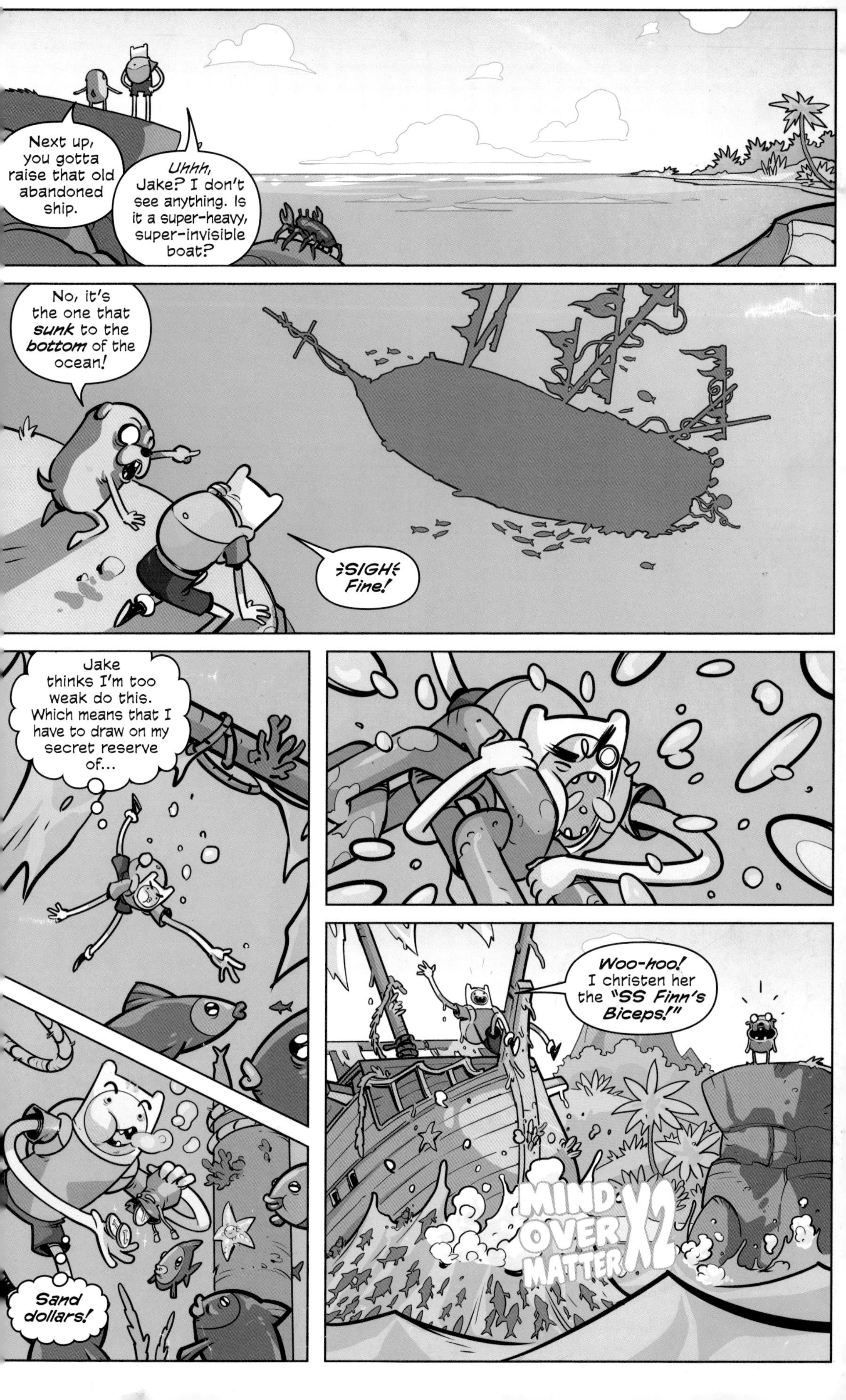
Next up, you gotta raise that old abandoned ship.
Uhhh, Jake? I don't see anything. Is it a super-heavy, super-invisible boat?
No, it's the one that sunk to the bottom of the ocean!
SIGH Fine!
Jake thinks I'm too weak do this. Which means that I have to draw on my secret reserve of...
Sand dollars!
Woo-hoo! I christen her the "SS Finn's Biceps!"
MIND OVER MATTER X2

"Lift that mountain!"
THWIP
Next!
CHA-THUNK
CHA-THUNK
BENCH PRESS
Urrrrgh!
TWO TONS

Oof!
2000lb

2000lb
scribble scribble
Hey, dude--

MIND OVER MATTER X3
WHOAAAAA!
2000lb
2lb
--UNFAIR!

PHEW! I am exhausted! Don't know how much longer we can keep doing this.
But it can't end in a tie! We need to know who's the strongest!
Wait! I know something that's even heavier than anything else we've tried. Something that I don't think anyone can lift!
Think I know exactly what you're talking about!
"The Ice King's spirits!"
Aw, Gunter. I'm so morose! Not even all these whimsical ice sculptures could cheer me up!
Melt 'em down. Just like all the others...
Wak!
KA-POW
Ice King, put down your sadness.
'Cause we're about to pick up the energy in here!
The Jake Suit?! What in the world?

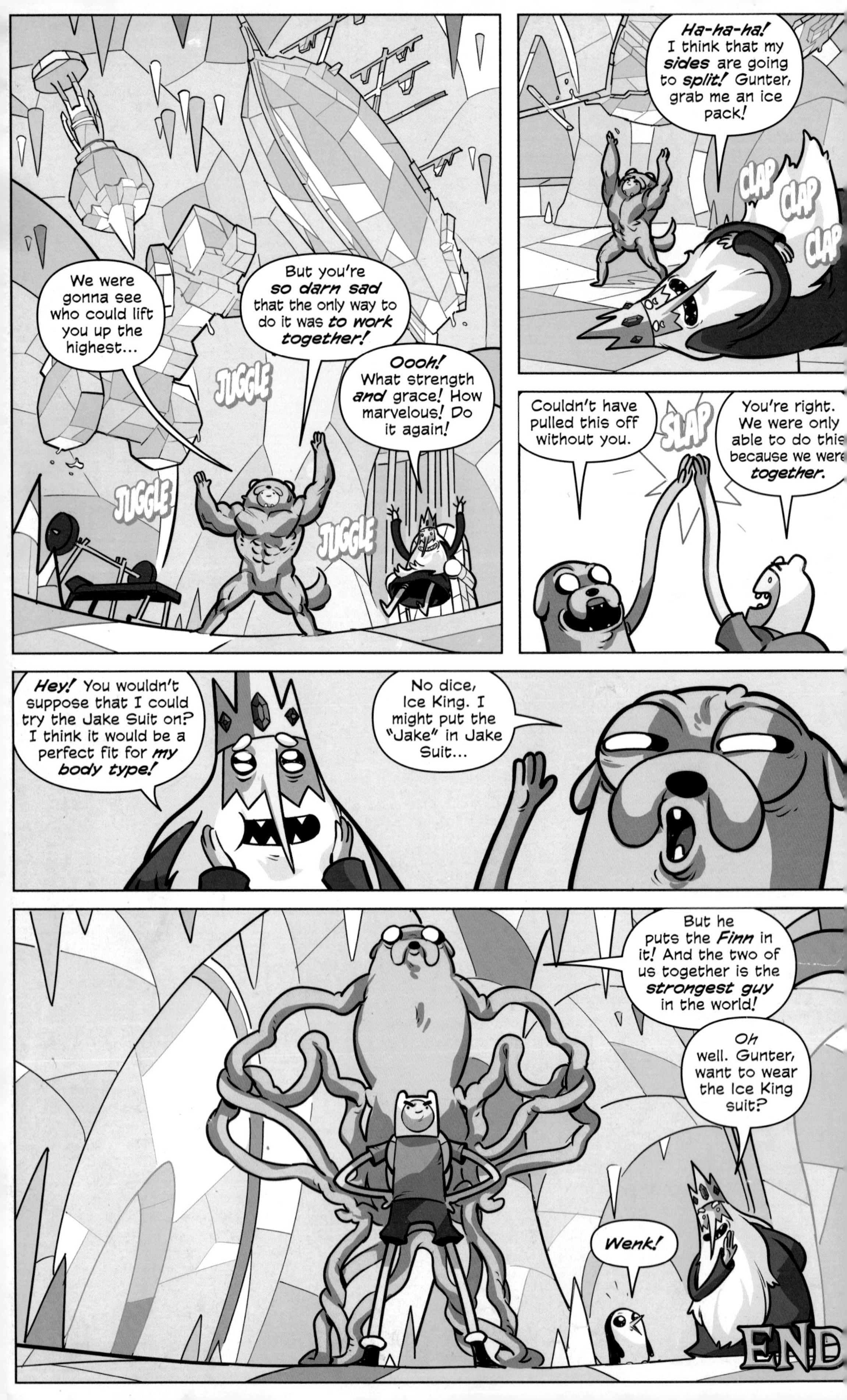
We were gonna see who could lift you up the highest...
But you're so darn sad that the only way to do it was to work together!
JUGGLE
JUGGLE
JUGGLE
Oooh! What strength and grace! How marvelous! Do it again!
Ha-ha-ha! I think that my sides are going to split! Gunter, grab me an ice pack!
CLAP
CLAP
CLAP
Couldn't have pulled this off without you.
SLAP
You're right. We were only able to do this because we were together.
Hey! You wouldn't suppose that I could try the Jake Suit on? I think it would be a perfect fit for my body type!
No dice, Ice King. I might put the "Jake" in Jake Suit...
But he puts the Finn in it! And the two of us together is the strongest guy in the world!
Oh well. Gunter, want to wear the Ice King suit?
Wenk!
END

A PYROHYDRA? **PARAMETRICAL!**
WATCH OUT, BUDDY! IT BREATHS **FIRE!**
BRING ON THE RAD GUYS!
WRITTEN BY JAI NITZ
ILLUSTRATED BY DEVMALYA PRAMANIK
COLORED BY TRIONA FARRELL
LETTERED BY ADITYA BIDIKAR
DUH, THAT'S WHAT PYROHYDRA MEANS. FIRE-BREATHING HYDRANT.
THAT MAKES SENSE.

LOOK AT ALL THIS LOOT. THERE'S GOTTA BE A NEW SWORD IN HERE.
OR A WAFFLE-MAKER.
SNIFF SNIFF SNIFF
HEY, IT'S TINY MANTICORE!
HE'S TRAPPED IN A JAR AGAIN.
WHAT'S UP, T.M.?
YEAH, WHAT'S THE WAFFLE STATUS AROUND HERE, DUDE?
RUN.
WHAT DID HE SAY?
I DUNNO. HE WAS FLYING AWAY TOO FAST.
HE SAID, "RUN."

DON JOHN THE FLAME LORD!
GULP
WHOOSH
HELP US, TINY MANTICORE! HELP US LIKE HOW WE HELPED YOU!
HA! TINY MANTICORE IS A COWARD!
A COWARD!

I'LL GO FIND THE ONE PERSON WHO CAN HELP ME DEFEAT DON JOHN AND SAVE FINN AND JAKE!

THE KING OF MARS HIMSELF!

NORMAL MAN!

OH, HEY, TINY MANTICORE. GOOD TO SEE YOU. DID YOU EVER BUY THAT BOAT?
THERE'S NO TIME FOR THAT! FINN AND JAKE ARE IN TROUBLE!
THEY'RE BEING HELD PRISONER BY DON JOHN THE FLAMELORD!

BUT I DON'T HAVE ANY POWERS ANYMORE. HOW CAN I HELP THEM?

HOW CAN WE NOT?

DON JOHN! WE'RE HERE TO RESCUE FINN AND JAKE!
MAGIC MAN AND TINY MANTICORE, TOGETHER AGAIN!
MAGIC MAN! HE'S TOO POWERFUL FOR ME TO STOP!
I THOUGHT HE WAS NORMAL MAN NOW.
YEAH. HE LOST ALL HIS POWERS.
GUYS!
YEAH! YOU SPOILED OUR RUSE!
HEH.
WELL, THAT WORKED OUT GREAT.
HOW WERE WE SUPPOSED TO KNOW?
WAIT, I HAVE AN IDEA.
OH DON JOOOOHN!

YES, KING OF MARS? YOU HAVE NO MAGICAL POWERS, WHAT CAN YOU OFFER ME?
I DON'T HAVE POWERS, BUT I HAVE THIS PAN OF CUPCAKES. THEY'RE WARM AND OOEY GOOEY.
CUPCAKES?

NOM
NOM NOM
NOM
NOM NOM

IT REALLY FEELS GOOD TO BE GOOD!
END.

FINN AND JAKE IN "CHOCK FULL O' STUFF" BY DAVID DEGRAND

SHOVE

SQUEEZE
PICKLES

STOMP
CRAM
STUFF

HA! HA!
HA! HA!

This meeting of the Easily Angered Mean Blob Monsters will now come to....
Hey! Those guys are mocking us!
Get 'em!

We didn't mean to offend you! We were just playin'!
AARGLE
DRAG
Next time let's play this game at home!
SLITHER
END

FINN VERSUS FINN
Written by Justin JORDAN
Illustrated by Mattia Di MEO
Colored by Joana LaFUENTE
Lettered by Jim CAMPBELL
JAAAA AAAAAAAAA AAAAAAAAAAAAA AAAAAAAAAAAAA AAAAAAAAAAAAA AAAAAAAAAAA AAAAAAKE.
WHAT'S WRONG, BUDDY?
I'M BOOOO OOOOOO OOOOOO OOOOOO OOORED.
WELL, I'D SAY YOU COULD PLAY THIS GAME WITH ME, BUT I THINK IT'S BROKEN. STUPID CURSED GAMES, ALWAYS UP IN MY BUSINESS.
BOOOO OOOOOO OOOOOO ORED.
WE COULD GO PUNCH SOMETHING. PUNCHING IS ALWAYS FUN.
I HATE TO SAY IT, JAKE, BUT IT FEELS LIKE...
PUNCHING HAS GOTTEN BORING.
IT'S JUST THE WAY I FEEL, DUDE.

NOW I'M BOOOOOOOORED OUTSIDE.
DON'T WORRY, FINN, I KNOW JUST THE PLACE TO GET YOU OUT OF YOUR NOT EVEN SLIGHTLY ANNOYING MALAISE. WE NEED TO GO SEE...

BIGGER ON THE INSIDE
WALLY WANDO, WARP WIZARD!

HE CAN TAKE US SOMEWHERE WE'VE NEVER SEEN TO FIGHT SOMETHING WE'VE NEVER FOUGHT. NOW THAT'S NOT BORING.

JAKE. ARE YOU HERE ABOUT THAT PICKLE HEIST?
NOT THIS TIME, WALLY WANDO, WARP WIZARD. I'M HERE BECAUSE MY BEST BUDDY FINN IS...
BOOOO OOOOOO OOOOOO RED.

YOU'RE RIGHT, JAKE, THIS IS THE WORST CASE OF--
--I'VE SEEN SINCE THE PICKLE HEIST GOT CANCELLED.
BOO OOOOOO OORED.
CAN YOU HELP WALLY WANDO, WARP WIZARD?

CAN AND SHALL!
THROUGH THIS WARP (COURTESY OF WALLY WANDO, WARP WIZARD, INC.) YOU WILL FIND THE GREATEST OPPONENTS YOU HAVE EVER FACED. UNMATCHED IN SKILL, UNPRECEDENTED IN PURE CHAOS. STEP THROUGH AND--

YEP, GOT IT. THANKS, WALLY WANDO, WARP WIZARD.
DUDE, IS THAT...
YES, BUDDY I THINK IT IS.
EVIL TWINS!
EVIL TWINS!
LET'S DO THIS.
LET'S DO THIS.

YOU ARE GOING DOWN, DUDE.
THEY SAY PERFECTLY SYMMETRICAL VIOLENCE NEVER SOLVED ANYTHING.
FEEL THE POWER OF THE FIST, EVIL FINN.
FEEL THE POWER OF *MY* FIST, EVIL FINN.

YOU ARE ONE FUNNY LOOKING DOG, EVIL JAKE.
Nuh-uh, EVIL JAKE.
Hah, I SAW THAT COMING A MILE AWAY, DUDE.
YES. BUT DID YOU SEE...
...*THIS* COMING.
Uh, YEAH.

DON'T LET EVIL FINN TRICK YOU.

WHAT DO YOU WANT, EVIL FINN?

YOU'RE EVIL FINN, NOT ME.
NO, DUDE, YOU'RE TOTALLY EVIL FINN.

IF YOU THINK I'M EVIL--
AND YOU THINK I'M EVIL--

MAYBE NEITHER OF US IS EVIL!

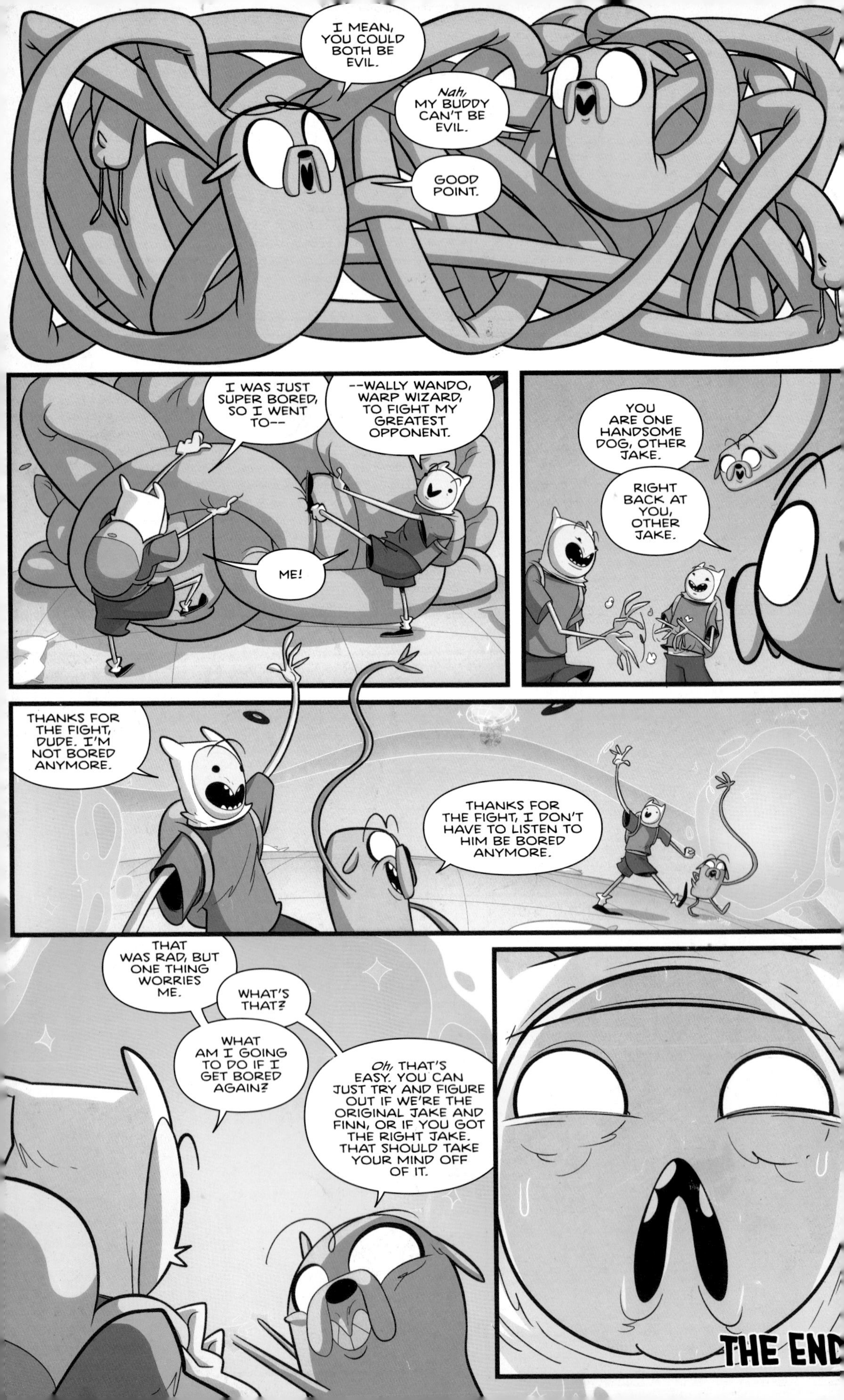
I MEAN, YOU COULD BOTH BE EVIL.
Nah, MY BUDDY CAN'T BE EVIL.
GOOD POINT.
I WAS JUST SUPER BORED, SO I WENT TO--
--WALLY WANDO, WARP WIZARD, TO FIGHT MY GREATEST OPPONENT.
ME!
YOU ARE ONE HANDSOME DOG, OTHER JAKE.
RIGHT BACK AT YOU, OTHER JAKE.
THANKS FOR THE FIGHT, DUDE. I'M NOT BORED ANYMORE.
THANKS FOR THE FIGHT, I DON'T HAVE TO LISTEN TO HIM BE BORED ANYMORE.
THAT WAS RAD, BUT ONE THING WORRIES ME.
WHAT'S THAT?
WHAT AM I GOING TO DO IF I GET BORED AGAIN?
Oh, THAT'S EASY. YOU CAN JUST TRY AND FIGURE OUT IF WE'RE THE ORIGINAL JAKE AND FINN, OR IF YOU GOT THE RIGHT JAKE. THAT SHOULD TAKE YOUR MIND OFF OF IT.
THE END

LOOK WHAT I GOT PRINCESS BUBBLEGUM FOR HER BIRTHDAY!
OH LOOK AT MINE!
HAPPY BIRTHDAY TO YOUUUUU!
UH, YOUR MAJESTY?
KNOCK KNOCK
P-B-M-O
WRITTEN BY CRYSTAL SKILLMAN & FRED VAN LENTE
ILLUSTRATED BY DANIELE DI NICUOLO
COLORED BY WALTER BAIAMONTE
LETTERED BY ADITYA BIDIKAR
MADAM, I DON'T MEAN TO INTERRUPT YOUR EXPERIMENTATION BUT YOU ARE MISSING YOUR OWN BIRTHDAY CELEBRATION!
ANOTHER BIRTHDAY? BLEGGH

TECHNICALLY IT'S JUST ANOTHER DAY I'M ALIVE. SO A BIRTHDAY IS JUST AS GOOD AS ANY OTHER DAY...
GAHFIREMON-FLAMEBALLS!

AH, MY CANDY EARS!
WHOA BMO? SLOW DOWN. WHAT'S WRONG?
FIREBALLS! MONSTERS! FLAMING MOTHBALLS! FINN! JAKE!
FINN AND JAKE HAVE BEEN TAKEN PRISONER BY THE FLAME PRINCESS?! THE FLAME KINGDOM WOULD DARE DO SUCH A THING?
THEY ARE BAD PEEPS?

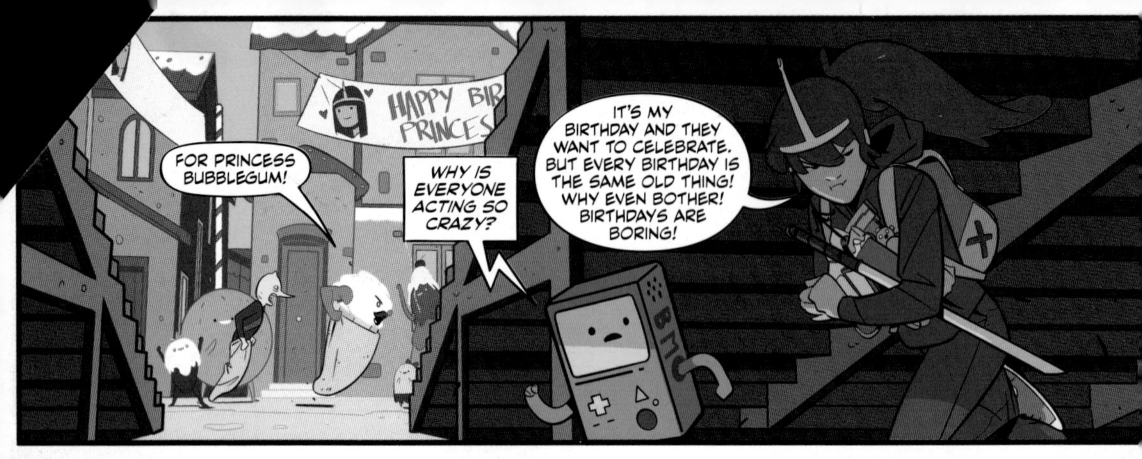
HAPPY BIR
PRINCES
FOR PRINCESS BUBBLEGUM!
WHY IS EVERYONE ACTING SO CRAZY?
IT'S MY BIRTHDAY AND THEY WANT TO CELEBRATE. BUT EVERY BIRTHDAY IS THE SAME OLD THING! WHY EVEN BOTHER! BIRTHDAYS ARE BORING!
BMO

EVEN BIRTHDAY DANCING?!!
ESPECIALLY BIRTHDAY DANCING.

SO, WHAT WERE YOU ALL DOING IN THE FIRE KINGDOM ANYWAY?
FINN SAID WE HAD A MISSION.
WHAT KIND OF MISSION?

IT WAS A SECRET.

OH, TURN LEFT HERE.
WHEN FINN AND JAKE AND I GO ON MISSION, THEY ASK ME TO NAVIGATE.
OH, THAT'S OKAY, I HAVE THIS BRAND NEW TOOL THAT IS PERFECT.
BMO IS BRAND NEW. BMO ALWAYS UPDATES.

WE GO THIS WAY.
WAIT! MY MAP TELLS ME WE DON'T WANT TO GO THROUGH HERE. TRUST ME.
IN THOSE MOUNTAINS THERE ARE MONSTERS. BIG, UGLY SMELLY ONES!

BMO LAUGHS IN THE FACE OF MONSTERS.
HA, HA!
BIG, SMELLY MONSTERS!
HA, HA!

RROOUAAR!
OH YOU WANT SOME? C'MERE!!

WHAT ARE YOU DOING? YOU'RE GETTING US IN MORE TROUBLE!
TROUBLE IS BMO'S MIDDLE NAME!
I THOUGHT IT WAS "M"!

NOW WE'RE EVEN FARTHER AWAY FROM THE FIRE KINGDOM!
YOU'RE SAFE, WELCOME! I PROTECT YOU, PRINCESS.

I CAN PROTECT MYSELF!
IT'S NOT ALL ABOUT YOU. WE NEED TO FIND FINN AND JAKE, DUH.

WHAT DO YOU THINK I'M DOING?!
GLUB GLUB
WAIT! WHAT WHAT'S THAT SOUND?

WE'RE HERE. THE SWAMP OF FRIENDSHIP!
OHHH BMO IS A GREAT CAPTAIN! SWAB THE DECK, SAILOR LADY!
NOW, WE HAVE TO BE QUIET ON THE LAGOON. SWAMP BATS CAN BE DANGEROUS WHEN WOKEN IN THE MIDDLE OF DREAMS ABOUT FOOD.
AND SWAMP BATS **ALWAYS** DREAM ABOUT FOOD.
OH, BMO WILL SING THEM TO SLEEP.
GO TO SLEEP, UGLY BATS! BMO IS NOT AFRAID OF YOU! BMO IS ON A MISSION! BMO AND PB COMING TO SAVE THE DAY! DUM DA DEE!

GAHH!
I TOLD YOU! NOW JUST LISTEN TO ME--
BMO ALWAYS LISTENS. BMO ALWAYS DOES WHAT'S BEST FOR YOU.
WHAT'S BEST FOR **ME** IS FOR **YOU** TO DO WHAT **I** SAY!
BMO THINKS YOU NEED TO COOL YOUR JETS.
AAAAHHH!!
WHEEEEE!!!

WE MADE IT! PRINCESS?
HELP!

PRINCESS!
BMO! SAVE YOURSELF!

NO.

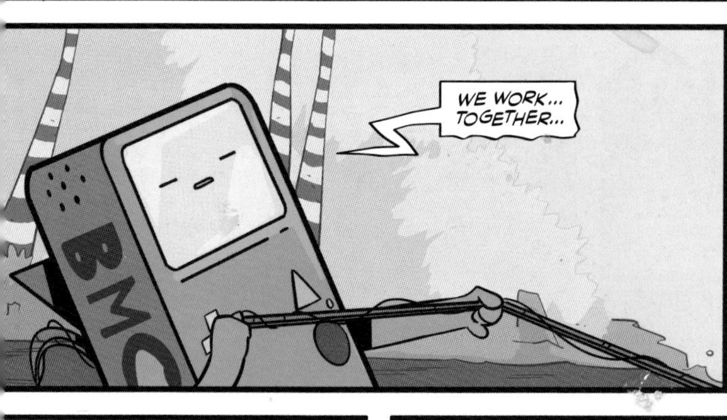
WE WORK... TOGETHER...

BMO!

OH, NO! BMO! ARE YOU OKAY?!

HOLD ON...

BWOOP
YOU'RE RIGHT. BIRTHDAYS ARE CRAZY.

CASTLE--
STORMED!
FRIENDS--
PREPARE TO
BE SAVED!

SURPRISE!!
WHHHAA...?

ARE YOU
SURPRISED, PB,
HUH, ARE YOU?
BUT--BMO
SHOWED
ME...

OH I SEE
WHAT HAPPENED
HERE...BMO...!
THESE FLAMES
WERE SUPPOSED TO
BE THE CANDLES FOR
YOUR CAKE--AND WHY
DO WE LOOK SO
SCARED?
FINN AND JAKE ARE
NOT SCARED--HAPPY!
BMO DOES NOT KNOW
WHAT SCARED IS!

THIS IS THE
MOST UNBORING
BIRTHDAY I'VE HAD IN
FOREVER...THANK
YOU...
...BMO!
HEY...BUT
I PLANNED
IT ALL...
BMO THE
BEST!

NOW WE
BIRTHDAY
DANCE!
END!

for the love of ooo
e jackson
I am Ready to find TRUE love, emphasis.
FINN
"filler Dude"
this is... my chase to...
I can't Read this LSP.
JAKE
"filler dude"
Dude.
this is gonna be hilarious.
Marceline
"filler dude"
I suppose this is an interesting social experiment...
P. B.
"filler dude"
I really don't want to be here.
BReakfast PRincess
"filler dude"
I am so Ready to find love.
Some Guy
"filler dude"
Oh man, thanks for including me. I'm—
BRADD
"filler dude"
"I'm here to fix the biggest mistake in my life"?
BRAD
"villain"
umm, I like, have a BF already??
Melissa
"villain"
I've been hurt, but my heart is like, totally open to the experience now.
LUMPY SPACE PRINCESS
host
Let's get this thing Started already!!

so like, I'm your host Lumpy Space Princess, and it's time for the GROUP DATE!!
I'm also a contestant so you BETTER talk to me!
NOW mingle!!!
Yo, actually, I'm gonna head out.
LADY'LL get mad jels if she finds out I've been "mingling".
bye dude
UGH! fine, bye already!
giggle
gasp!
hello there...
um, ew.
oh my glob, Melissa and BRad are just the WORST.
I'm gonna go bust thei lumps!
LSP
bachelorette

oh hey LSP... I thought it'd be nice if we could-
GLOB OFF I'm busy!
BRAD, could I steal you away?
um... we're like, in the middle of something, LSP?
SHUT UP MELISSA!! YOU'RE NOT here FOR the RIGHT REASONS!
Come on, Brad- it's time FOR the lumpin' SOLO DATE!
can we leave now?
NO!!

So like, the thing is I'm really—
VRRRR
RRRT!
—into you—
—It's Melissa—
VRRRRR
RRRT!
—Keeping us apart
why are you crying?
oh Brad, you're a dumb jerk, but I think we have like, something real...
take my
TOKEN of OOOFECTION
this is a piece of trash.
BRAD
"hot jerk"

now everyone shut your glob!
CLANK
CLANK
it's time for MY ceremony!!
one for you~
oh, like, thanks?
for you~
and the final one...
goes to BRADD!
sweet
The rest of you are like, big losers.
SO SCRAM!
good luck Finn!
haha he needs it
I thought... it was my time for love...
This was so dumb.
It's so lumping hard, breaking hearts~
uh, LSP?

thanks, I think, but I gotta go uh... change BMO's battery. Later!
WHAT
YOU CAN'T JUST-
Yeah, we're leaving too. It's date night~
TOSS
NO! We need the dramatic tension o
our love triangle fo
the season's main thrust!
oh glob, I'll never find love...
I'll stick around, LSP...
ugh, you're just the lousy filler dude.
I guess... I'm the only on
in OOO ready for true love...
ooo of looove
I'm a globbing creative genius.
the END

WHERE THE SLIME LIVE
Written & Illustrated by Steve SEELEY
Lettered by Jim CAMPBELL
RAH! HOW DARE YOU!
HOW DARE YOU ENTER MY REALM, THE PLACE WHERE THE SLIME LIVE...
...AND STEAL FROM MY SON, PRINCE POUPEE, FUTURE RULER OF THIS WORLD!
SUCH LACK OF RESPECT!
AND TO AWAKEN ME, SUPREME LORD YUCK, MASTER OF CRUD, GOD OF GOO... ON THE 48TH DAY OF MY SLIMBER TO STEAL WHAT? POUPEE'S NEW HAT?
HAT? YOU MEAN THE SLIME PRINCESS' STOLEN CROWN?
ALSO, THERE'S NO SUCH THING AS A SLIME KING. SORRY, MAN.

WHAT IS SLIMBER YOU ASK?
NOPE.
NOT WHAT I SAID.
AH, YES, IT IS A SLIME-INDUCED SLUMBER OF INCREDIBLE FILTH.
AS WE SLIME SLEEP IN THE SCUM OF OUR ENEMIES WE ARE BATHED IN THE SLUDGE OF A THOUSAND VICTORIES.
VICTORIES THAT LET US MIMIC THOSE WHO WE HAVE BESTED, TO BECOME THE ULTIMATE MASTERS OF OOZING DISGUISE!
DO YOU RECOGNIZE THIS HEAD? THIS POOR LOSER?
NO? TOO BAD!
THAT IS ON YOU AND YOUR SM MISSHAPEN NON-SLIME BRAINS!

OF COURSE YOU KNOW *THIS FACE?!*
OLD JAMMIE?
ELDER OF THE CLOUD CHAMBER?!
HE RECENTLY CRIED DEFEAT AT MY SLIMY HANDS!
R *THIS* ONE?!
NOPE, JUST DON'T CARE.
I TAKE YOUR SILENCE AS EITHER YOUR UTTER STUPIDITY OR YOUR IMPENDING DEFEAT... OR PERHAPS BOTH! *HUZZAH!* THE SLIME IS WINNING.

SERIOUSLY? COME ON! AND WHAT ABOUT THIS GUY? EH...?
SURELY YOU KNOW--
HEY, JAKE, DID HE REALLY SAY HIS KID'S NAME WAS POO PEE?
YEAH, I THINK SO, MAN.
HEHE... POO PEE!
HAHAHA!
GROSS.
COOL "HAT," THOUGH!
THE EN

B-MAX
by anoosha syed
BMO
hop!
keep the change!
BMO
Princess Bubblegum!
I need your help!
What do you need ya cutie?
cue the MONTAGE MUSIC!
That's the problem PB, I'm just too cute for my own good! No one wants a tiny robot on any adventures.
Make me a buff robot bod so I can fight like Finn and Jake!
Hmm... a tech upgrade you say? I got just what you need.

There!
That should do it!
I took the liberty of adding a few upgrades to your suit, nothing bananas.
Let me see, let me see!

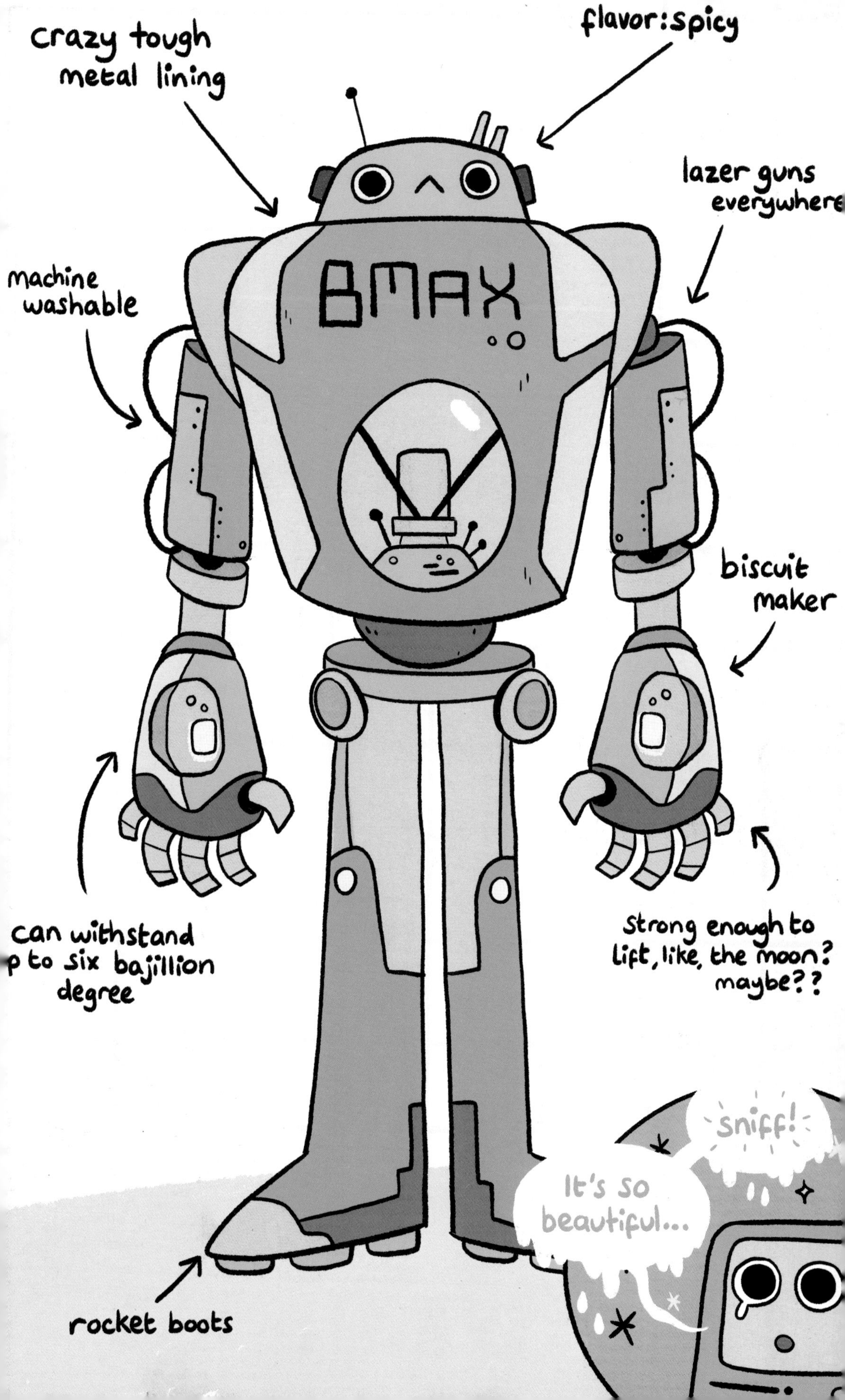
crazy tough
metal lining
flavor:spicy
lazer guns
everywhere
BMAX
machine
washable
biscuit
maker
can withstand
p to six bajillion
degree
strong enough to
lift, like, the moon?
maybe??
rocket boots
sniff!
It's so
beautiful...

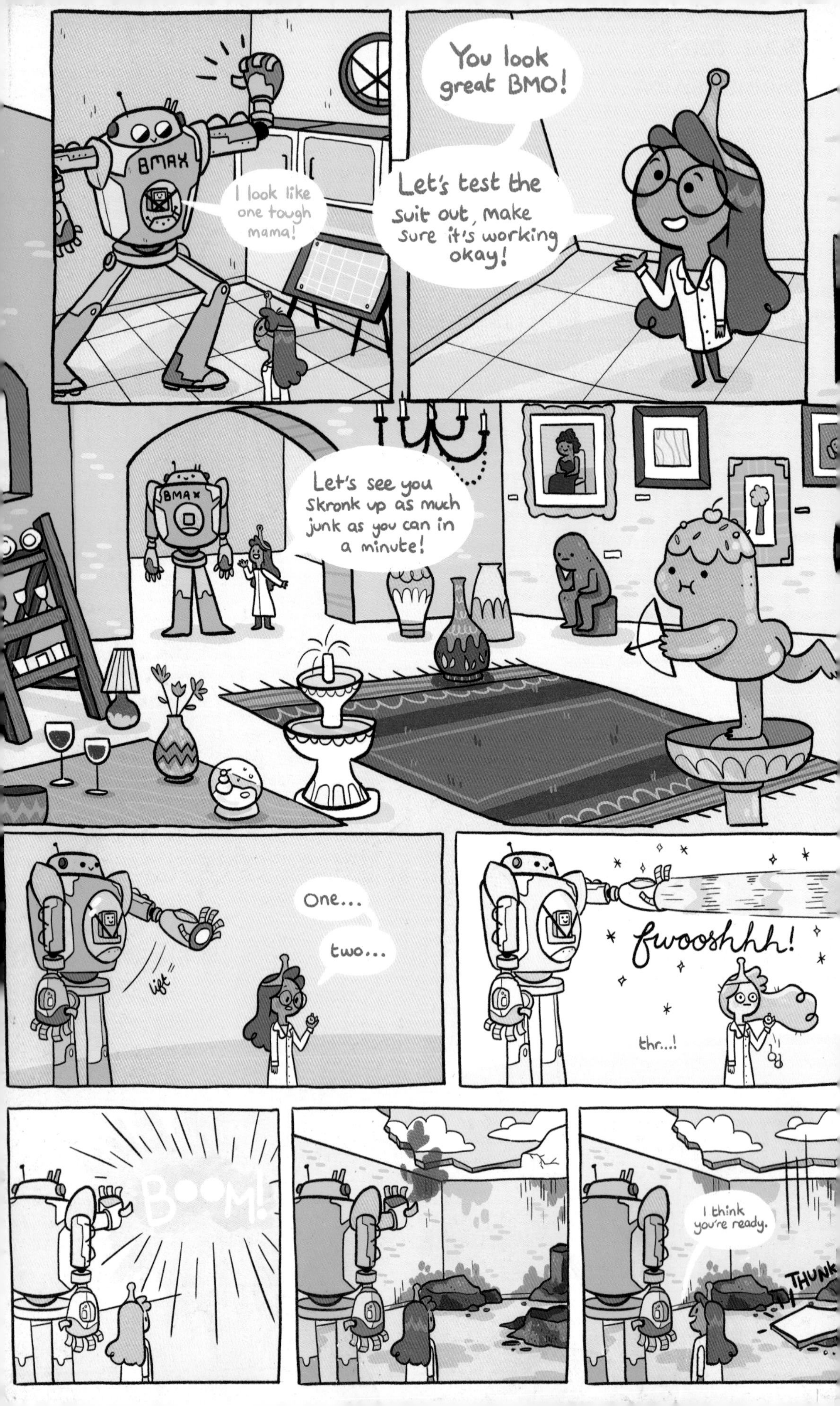
BMAX
I look like one tough mama!
You look great BMO!
Let's test the suit out, make sure it's working okay!
BMAX
Let's see you skronk up as much junk as you can in a minute!
lift
One...
two...
fwooshhh!
thr...!
BOOM!
I think you're ready.
THUNK

Thanks Princess! I am now off to kick some bad guy tooshie!
The cave should be just around the corner.
I heard the monster guarding the treasure is bonkers tough, but I think we can take it down with your new bot-bod.
Don't worry, I'll give him a wa-pow! and a ka-chop! and a pew-pew-pew!
yeah that slimy dude won't stand a chance!
Speaking of slimy dudes...
GRRR...

Fight!
FINN & JAKE
VS
MONSTER DUDE

AAAARGHH...!

SPLAT!

I don't think we're doing so good, Jake.
BMAX
OH NO! I will save you guys!
POW!
WHOOP!
KICK

Oh wait! I've got it!
EJECT!
EJECT!
BMO
BMAX
AARRRGH!
AAAAA AAOoh my glob!
GRAB
you're just too cute!
sneak sneak
Thanks BMo!
the end!

THE THUMB-DERDOME

WRITTEN AND ILLUSTRATED BY MARIE ENGER

WELCOME TO THE...
THUMB-DER DOME!!
WOAH!
RIGHT?
EIGHT THUMBS ENTER!
HA! THIS IS CRAZY!
TWO THUMBS LEAVE!

ALRIGHT, GUYS!
I WANT A GOOD CLEAN FIGHT!
REMEMBER WHERE YOU ARE--
--THIS IS THE THUMB-DER-DOME!
DING! DING! DING!
SLAM
THUMP
ONE!!
TWO!!
THREE!!

YOU! ARE!
OUTTA HERE!
BOOT
SNIFF!
MISS
BIFF
ONE!!
TWO!!
THREE!!
NEXT!
SWIPE
SMASH
CITIZENS OF OOO!

WE HAVE A WINNER!!
BOOOHHH HOOO...

BUT...
...WE DO NOT HAVE A VICTOR.
WHU?
OH...
OH... NO...

FORGED NOT FROM DIRT AND MUD, BUT FROM WIRES AND METAL...

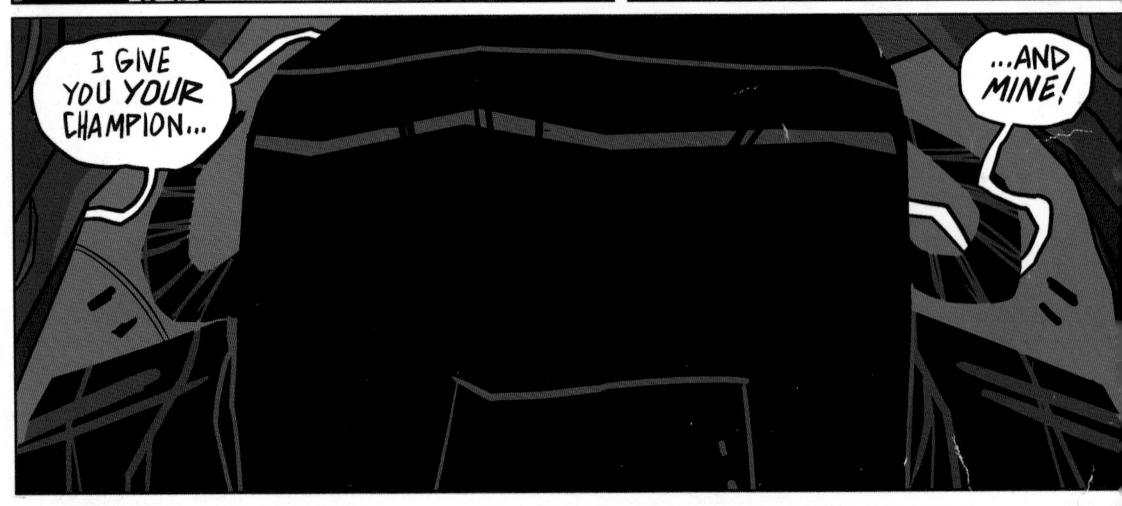
I GIVE YOU YOUR CHAMPION...
...AND MINE!

"AUNTY" PHALANGES!!
WAIT... IS THAT?
"GO" BMOOO!!
WELL,
WELL,
WELL.
WHUH?
AREN'T WE A PAIR.
WAIT!
OH MY GLOB.
IT CAN'T BE!
THIS...
...IS...
...A...
...RULES VIOLATION!
RULES?

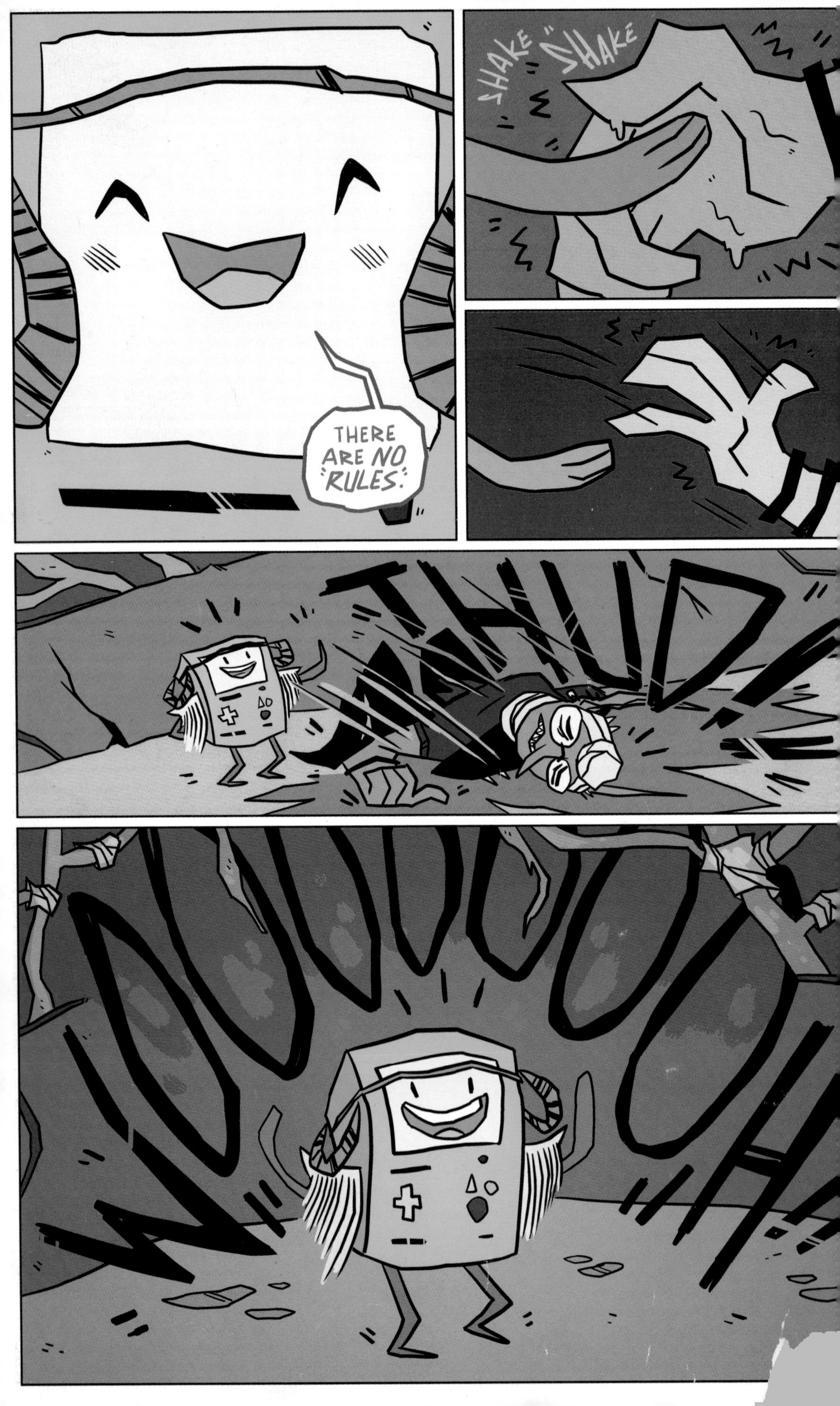
THERE ARE NO RULES.
SHAKE SHAKE
THUD
NOOOOOOH

GREAT JOB, BMO!
YAY!
BMO!
THAT WAS WILD!
I THOUGHT THESE GOBLINS WERE ALL SORTS OF MILD!
BUT, YOU GOTTA TELL ME--
--HOW'D YOU WIN AGAINST THAT BIG GOB?
THAT IS SO EASY!

I HAVE NO THUMBS!!
END

"THE GREAT CRABBY-BEAST" BY JENNA AYOUB
AS THE CRABBY-BEAST LOOMS OVER THE CRUMBLING SAND CASTLE...
...WHO WILL SAVE PRINCESS BUBBLEGUM
HI-YAHHHH!
OH GLOB!
RAH! RAH! RAH!
FINN!
OHNOOOOOOOOOOOOOOo!
TELL HIM TO ASK ME NICELY.
LET HIM GO, BEAST!
HA HA!
HA HA!
END

MIGHTIER Than The FIST!
Stop right there Ninja Pete and face me!
YEA! Gimme my body back!
YOU think YOU CAN DEFEAT ME FINN AND JAKE?!
I AM NINJA PETE!
FACE MY CLUBBIN FEET!!!
WUD
WUD
WUD
WUD
WUD
WUD
WUD
JAKE his attack is too POWERFUL! what do I do?!
Spider bus! My tongue is a spider bus!
DIP-LOW KICK!
AW JEEZ there I go.
MAN JAKE you didn't even back me up bro!
I'm just a head!

I thought I had some sick fighting moves but just got served!
Maybe you can find a fighting master, they're always of mountains and stuff...
hmm,
LATER
f o o o o s h
w W o o o o sh
This is body of BLOOR tha JUDO MOUNTAIN GIANT, defeated by my homie MASTER FUT PWR!
MASTER OF THE HYPER CHOP
WAP!
and the BACK SIZZLING DROP-KICK
oooooooh

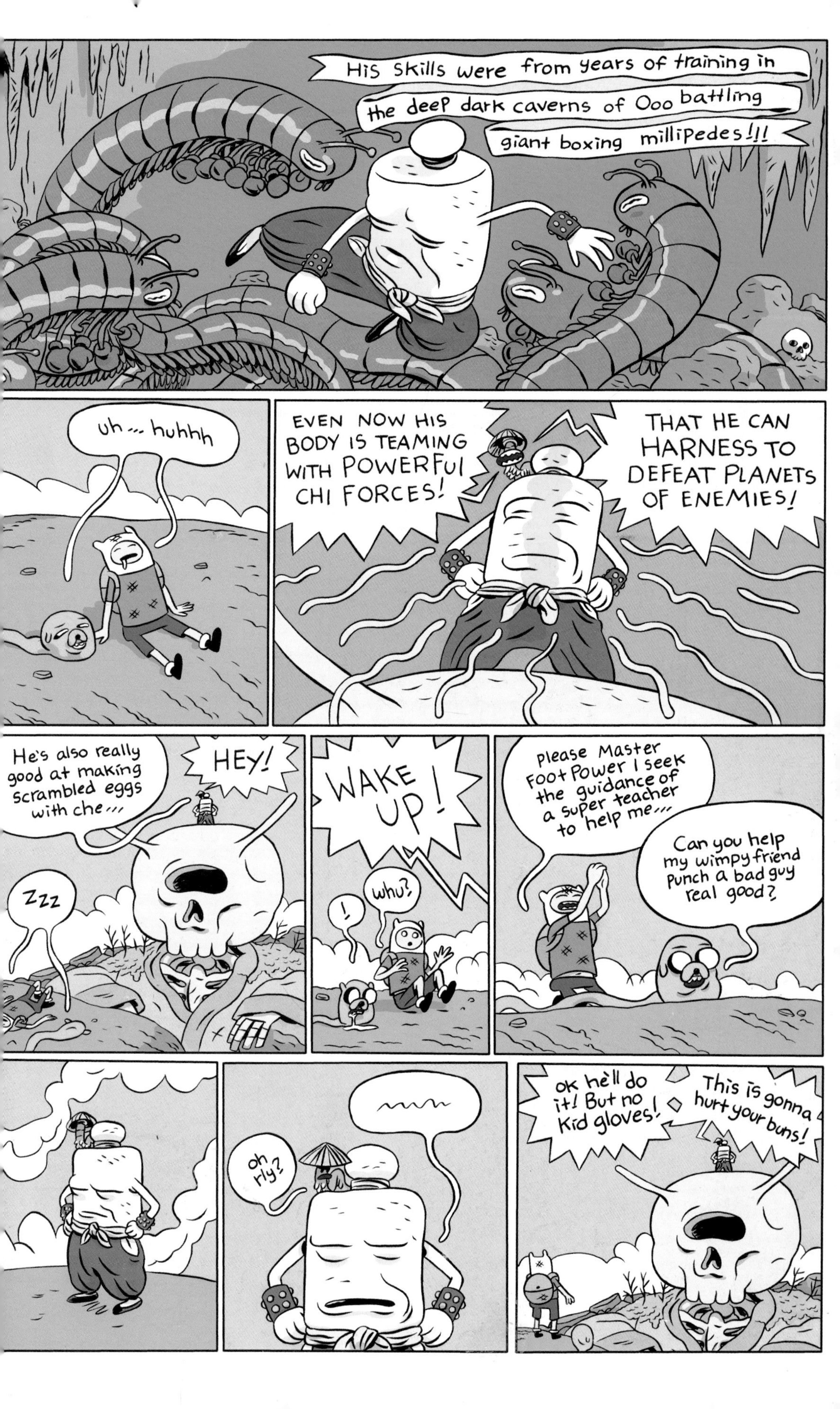

His skills were from years of training in
the deep dark caverns of Ooo battling
giant boxing millipedes!!!
uh... huhhh
EVEN NOW HIS BODY IS TEAMING WITH POWERFUL CHI FORCES!
THAT HE CAN HARNESS TO DEFEAT PLANETS OF ENEMIES!
He's also really good at making scrambled eggs with che...
HEY!
Zzz
WAKE UP!
!
whu?
please Master Foot Power I seek the guidance of a super teacher to help me...
Can you help my wimpy friend punch a bad guy real good?
oh rly?
ok he'll do it! But no kid gloves!
This is gonna hurt your buns!

BEGIN!
groan
groan
groan
several montages later...
GROAN!
GROOOAN!
AAAAH
Think warm thoughts buddy!
weeeeeee
?

weeeee
ha ha
!
WOK
what the ?! what?!
oh no! show me where it hurts!
Waaaaaaaaaa
Jigs up! You're scamming my friend with this super hard training!
Now he's more down in the dumps than ever!
blubber
NO NO, we just wanted to help!
MFP did beat Bloor The Judo Mountain Giant! Just not with his fists...
He always wanted to be a master fighter but his skin is super soft. We used to shadow box in the caves. But after a while he started to think he might actually be a master fighter.
I didn't want to crush his dreams or let him get crushed by Bloor The Judo mountain giant!
If you really want to know how to defeat Finn's opponents without Finn getting hurt I'll tell you the secret technique.
guard it with your life!

NINJA PETE!
?
FACE MY FRIEND!
I still feel pretty sore Jake,
grrr
You really want more of this Finn the Losing?!
you got this one friendo!
ahem
BEHOLD MASTER FINN! expert at the HYPER NOSE POKE, KNEE OF EXPLODING DESTINY and DIVING STRIKE OF FLAMING EAGLE OF WINNING!!!
YA
WOOSH!
KICK!
oooooooh!
Forged from crushing training under MASTER FUT PWR and the Boxing Millipede in the frozen peaks of Mount Bloor, Finn learned all the styles of assault!
POW
YAAAWN.
Finn is the greatest and my friend and we do a lot of stuff together like adventures and also lunch...
Z
Well we're buddies again and buddier than ever!
the buddliest!
Best of all I got all these cool fighting moves!
rrrright.
THE END

BROKEN
Written & Illustrated by Bethany SELLERS
Colored by Joana LaFUENTE
Lettered by Jim CAMPBELL
HEY, DON'T RUN OFF FAR, OKAY?
I WON'T!
C'MON, HAMBO, I THINK I SAW A SQUIRREL BACK HERE!
KSHH
RIP

WHA--

SIMON!
MARCELINE?!

MARCELINE, WHAT'S WRONG?

S-SIMON, I...I BROKE HAMBO.

Oh...

I'M S-SORRY!
AWW, HEY NOW, IT'S OKAY! YOU DON'T NEED TO APOLOGIZE.

SEE? YOU DIDN'T BREAK HAMBO; HE JUST HAS A LITTLE TEAR, THAT'S ALL! WE'LL GET THAT FIXED RIGHT UP!
R-REALLY?
Sniff
DEFINITELY!
ALTHOUGH... FIRST WE'LL HAVE TO FIND A NEEDLE AND SOME THREAD.
...AND I SHOULD PROBABLY LEARN HOW TO ACTUALLY SEW.
LATER.
HERE WE GO! I'M SURE WE'LL FIND SOMETHING HERE.
Hmm, SEWING SUPPLIES, SEWING SUPPLIES...
YOU HAVING ANY LUCK, MARCELINE?
NOPE!
WE'RE GETTING CLOSE, MARCY, I CAN SMELL IT! AAAAAND...
Gah, RATS! THOSE ARE RATS! LOTS OF RATS!
EEEWW!

O-OKAY, LET'S CHECK UNDER THE BED NEXT...

C'MOOON, I KNOW YOU'RE AROUND HERE SOMEWHERE.
...PLEASE DON'T LET THERE BE MORE RATS.

BINGO! WE DID IT, MARCY!
HOORAY!

...

Uh... MARCY, REMEMBER WHAT I TOLD YOU ABOUT ***STEALING?***
THAT IT'S WRONG AND YOU SHOULDN'T DO IT?
YEP, THAT'S IT.

IS THIS LIKE WHEN YOU SAY, *'DO AS I SAY AND NOT AS I DO'*, SIMON?
I THINK YOU'RE GETTING TO BE A LITTLE TOO SMART FOR MY OWN GOOD.

DON'T YOU ORRY, HAMBO, E'LL HAVE YOU XED UP IN NO TIME!
SIMON, DO YOU KNOW WHAT YOU'RE DOING?
SURE, WHY NOT? IT CAN'T BE THAT HARD, RIGHT?
TITCH STITCH STITCH
POKE
OW!
STITCH STITCH STITCH

OKAY, MARCY, ARE YOU READY?
TA-DA! GOOD AS NEW!
...SORT OF.

HE'S PERFECT! THANK YOU, SIMON!
YOU'RE WELCOME, SWEETIE.
AND YOU DOUBTED ME!
Nuh-uh! HAHAHA!
YOU KNOW...THIS REMINDS ME OF SOMETHING MY MOTHER TOLD ME WHEN I WAS, oh... A LITTLE OLDER THAN YOU, I THINK.
SHE SAID THAT NO MATTER HOW BROKEN SOMETHING MAY BE, THERE WILL ALWAYS BE A WAY TO FIX IT AGAIN.
AND, WELL... I WANT YOU TO REMEMBER THAT, OKAY, MARCY?
OKAY, SIMON!
THE EN

HE BUMMER STORY OF CHOOSE GOOSE
Written by Leah WILLIAMS
Illustrated by Ryan JAMPOLE
Colored by Joana LaFUENTE
Lettered by Jim CAMPBELL
There once was a gosling named Chauncey. Noble and proud was he.
Feather of pearl,
His father an Earl,
He came from a rich family.

When gosling became gander,
Young Chauncey chose to meander.
He left a home so dear,
For a forest near,
In search of ways to make his family richer.
He traveled through plains and swamps of Ooo,
When he tired of walking he flew.
THANK YOU THANK YOU THANK YOU THANK YOU THANK YOU THANK YOU THANK YOU
He made new friends,
Crashed in their dens,
And soon enough, Chauncey knew--

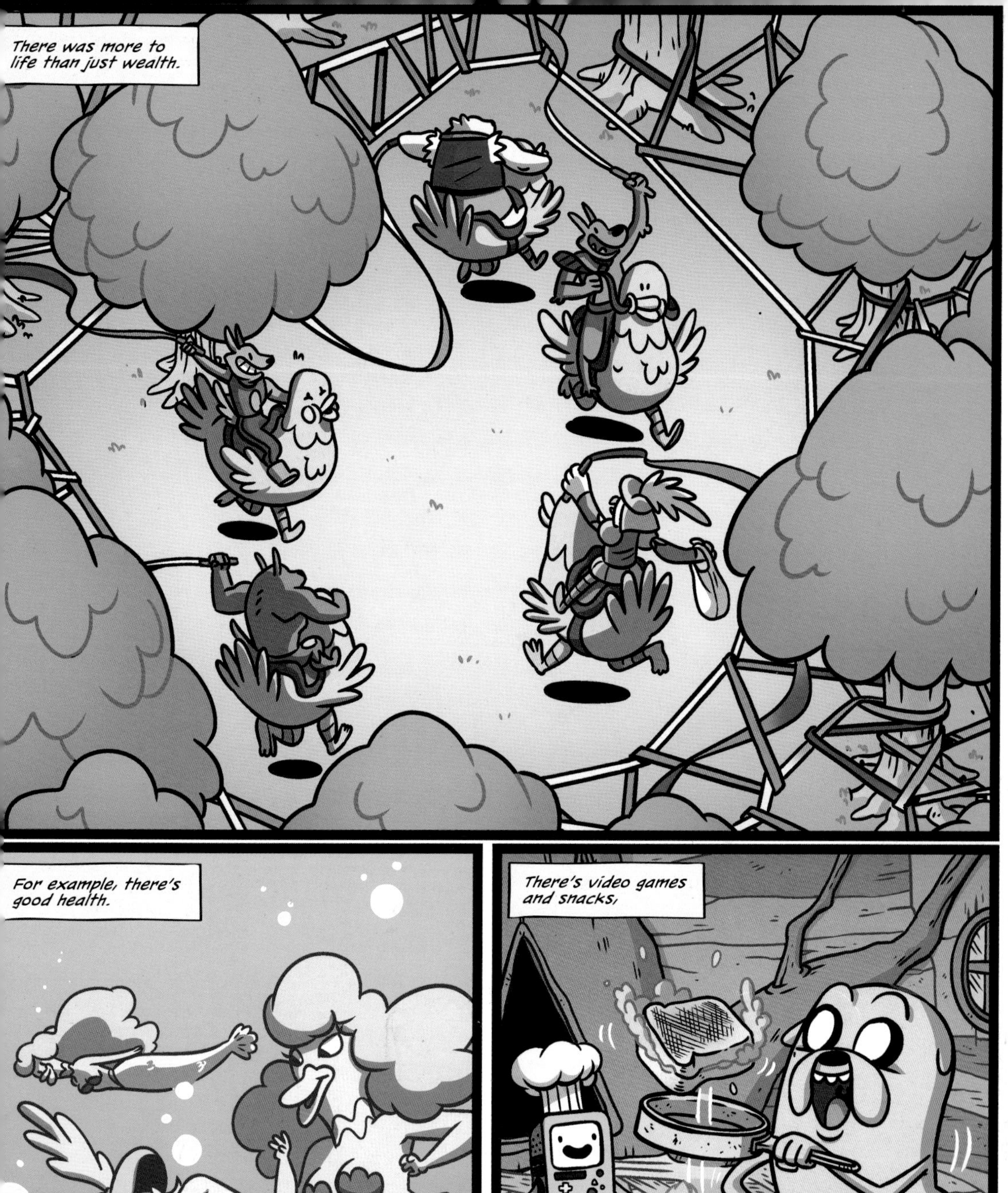
There was more to life than just wealth.

For example, there's good health.

There's video games and snacks,

There's best friends and long naps.
But soon came the day when Chauncey's new conscience rebelled--

One day while out playing, Chauncey spotted bloodberries at the edge of a clearing. Worth their weight in gold, Bloodberries are a boon to be sold.
TURN BACK
TURN BACK
STAY AWAY
KEEP OUT
STAY AWAY
So he saddled his pigeon and ignored every warning.
NOW YOU'RE TRESPASSING
STAY AWAY
STAY AWAY
KEEP OUT
DUDE! THAT'S NOT COOL!
STOP!
CHAUNCEY, WAIT--
DO YOU WANT TO BE CURSED BY A WITCH? BECAUSE THIS IS HOW FOLKS GET CURSED BY WITCHES.

When his bag was ripe to bursting, what happened next was the worst thing.
A wizened crone appeared, Air crackling with magic as she neared. With a devious smirk, her hand on a dirk-- She looked super weird.
YOUNG BIRD--YOU ARE TRESPASSING ON MY PROPERTY.
Uh. I NEED A FEW MORE OF THESE. I'LL JUST BE A SEC.

'Ah, ah'--the crone replied.
ON MY LAND, WE SPEAK IN RHYME.
THAT'S SILLY.

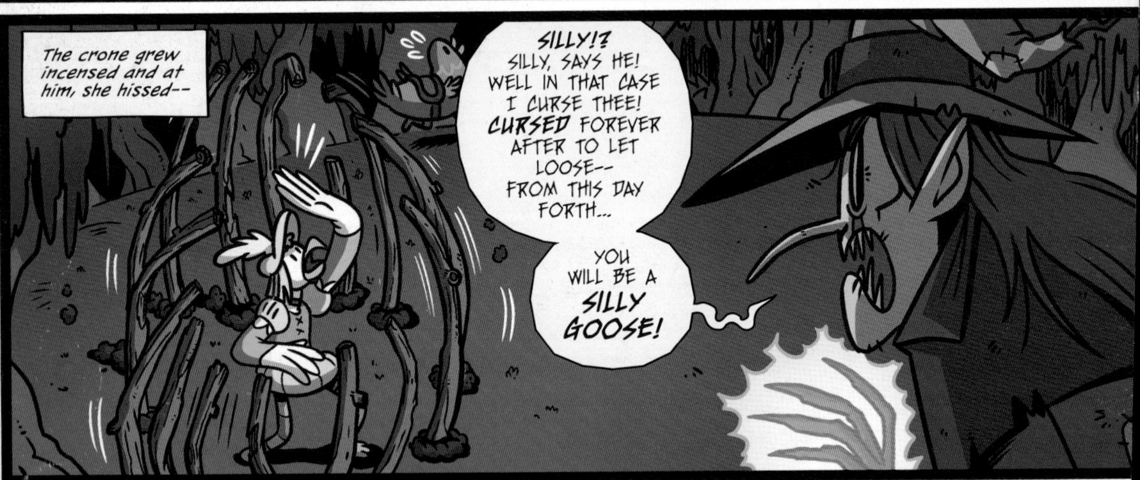
The crone grew incensed and at him, she hissed--
SILLY!? SILLY, SAYS HE! WELL IN THAT CASE I CURSE THEE! CURSED FOREVER AFTER TO LET LOOSE-- FROM THIS DAY FORTH...
YOU WILL BE A SILLY GOOSE!

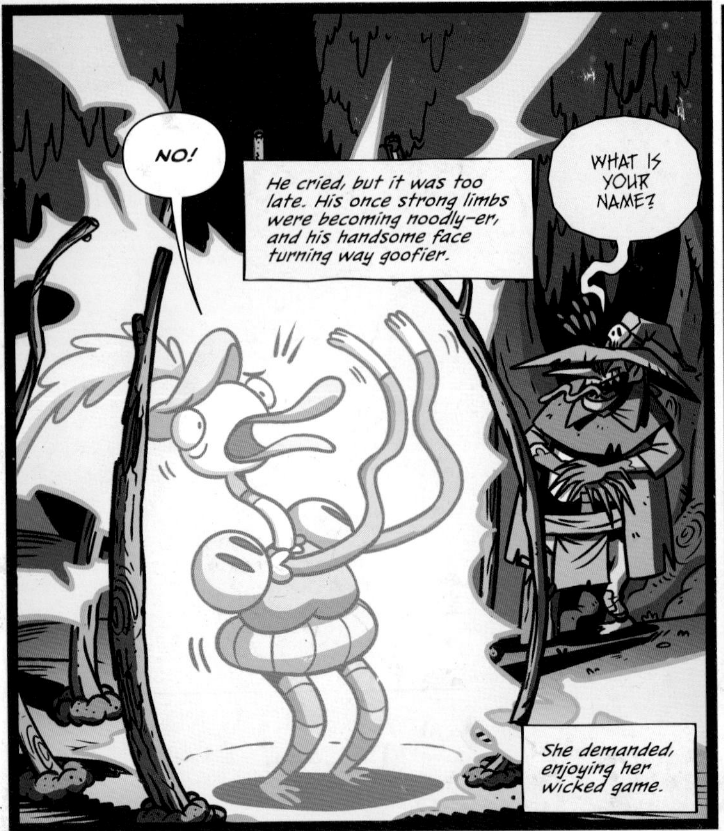
NO!
He cried, but it was too late. His once strong limbs were becoming noodly-er, and his handsome face turning way goofier.
WHAT IS YOUR NAME?
She demanded, enjoying her wicked game.

CHAUNCEY GOOSE!
Said he proudly.
A GOOSE'S NAME IS HIS EVERYTHING-- HIS FAMILY AND HISTORY, IDENTITY, BELONGING, A PORTEND, A WARNING, A MARK OF HIS ROYALTY--
I AM CHAUNCEY GOOSE!
He added fiercely

WHO ARE YOU?
Asked the crone once more.
ARE YOU STILL CHAUNCEY? ARE YOU SUUUUURE?
I'M-- I'M--
CH-CHOOSE GOOSE!
He cried, to his horror.
He fled in tears and terror.
MONTHS LATER.
Few can stand a Silly Goose's company. (It's hard for them to take anything seriously.)
RIP
He couldn't go home,
His usefulness to his family outgrown,
So, cursed to rhyme, Choose Goose then tried his wing at singing.

Booed from the stage, and dodging groceries thrown in rage,
Choose Goose realized he'd only ever been good at one thing.

Buying and selling.
As a cursed bird, this proud capitalist had found his final cage.

As for the crone who first cursed the rhyming merchant, No one knows where she went.
No one, that is, except me.

With Goose manor missing an heir, it was easy for this crone to usurp the Goose throne.
And that, younglings, is the tale of why I cursed he.
(TL;DR: he had it coming)
Oh, and PS: if any of you dorks wonder if my tale be true, well--I'll leave the matter of that up to you.
THE EN

COSMO
CUSTODIAN
Written & Illustrated by
Ian HERRING

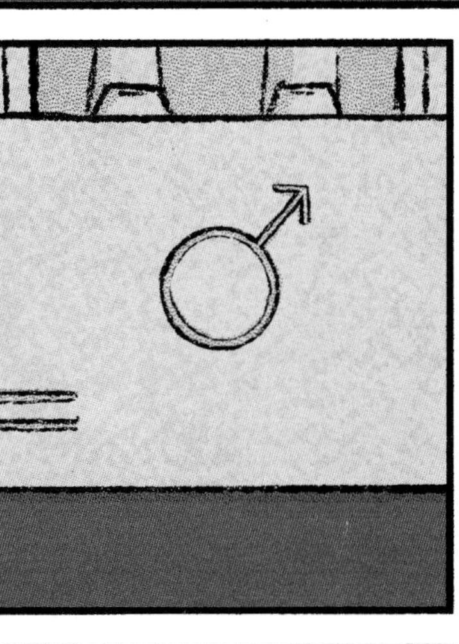

Coooooooooooooooooooooooo

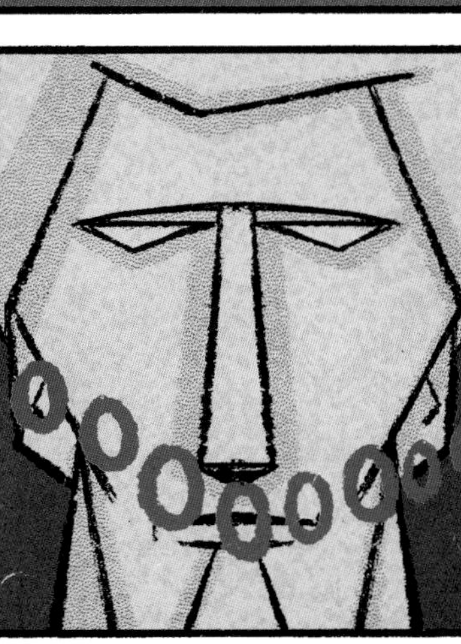

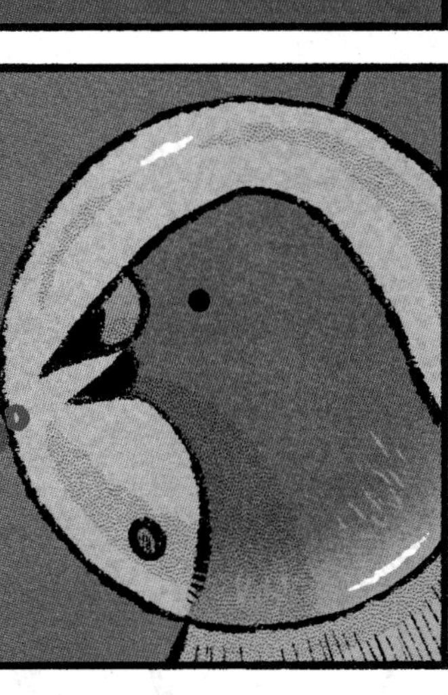

SHOooOO

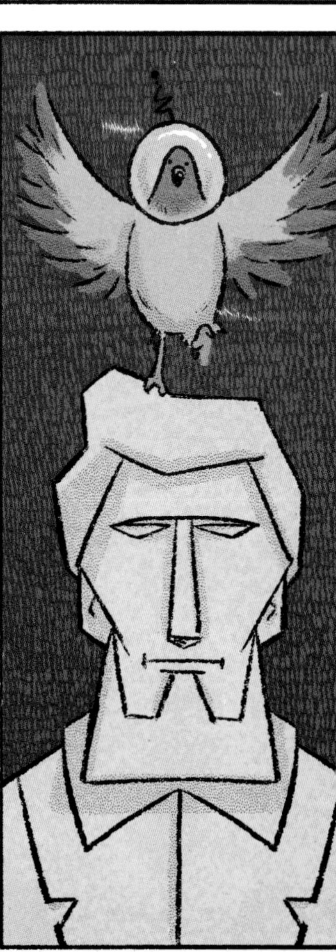

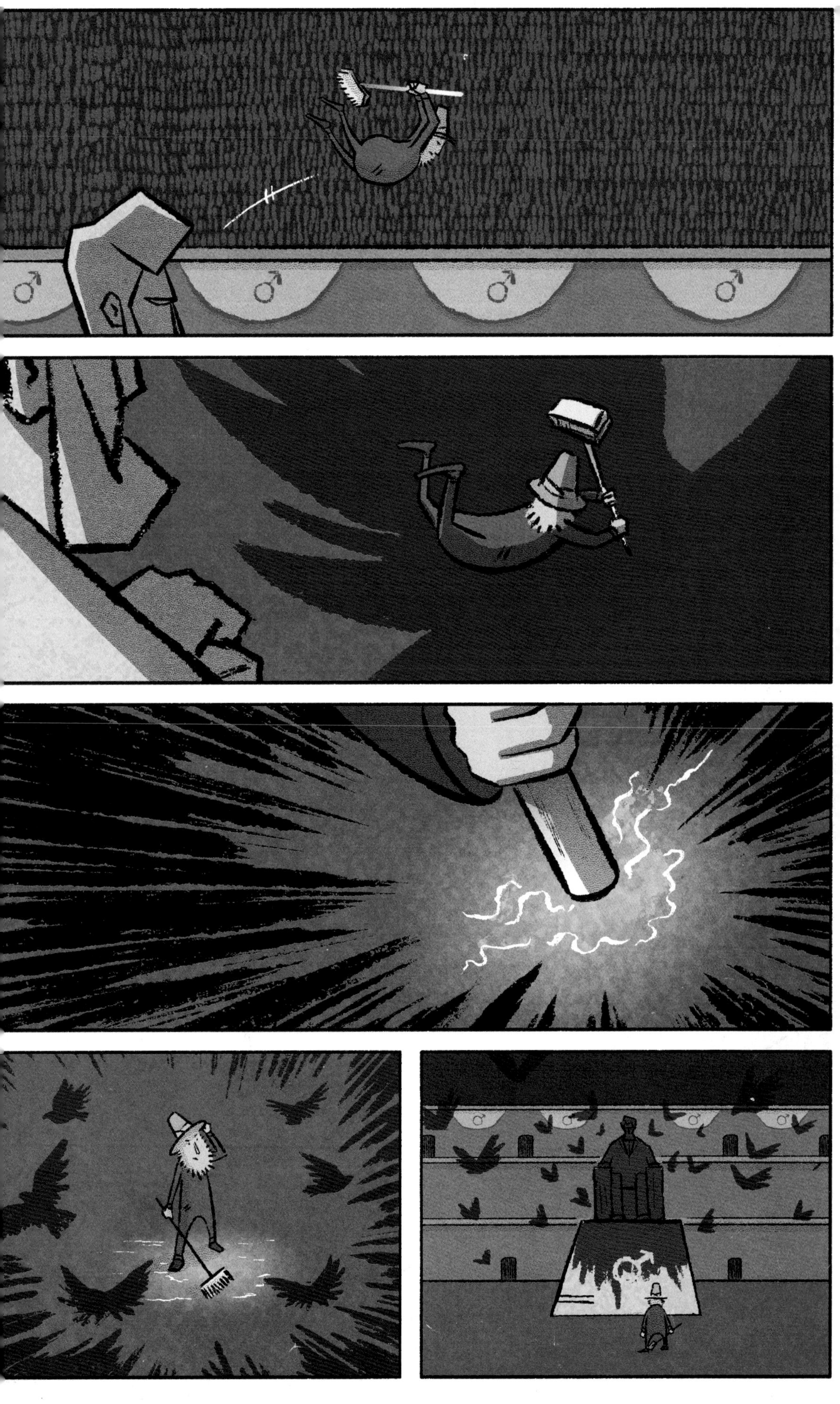

AV ROOM

CLICK

THE END

TRAINING DAY

The final section of your Banana Guard annual review training is on this here video.

Now...let's see... AH! PLAY!

As a member of the Banana Guard Team....

It's up to you...

...To BE READY!

Banana Guards are the Eyes & Ears of the Candy Kingdom.

Remember to check for dangers and hazards.
CK Coordinator Banana Guard

SOME DANGERS MAY INCLUDE

Remember A.B.E. Always-Be-Alert!
A • Always
B • Be
E • Alert

Danger is all around.
BONK!
oof!

Be on the lookout for suspicious behavior.

Remember...
The Candy Kingdom...
...is counting...
ON YOU!!!
STOP

Well done. Any Questions?

COVER GALLERY

Issue #13 Main Cover

KIM MYATT

Issue #13 Subscription Cover

JORGE MONLONGO

Issue #13 Variant Cover

SEAN CHEN WITH COLORS BY WHITNEY COGAR

Issue #14 Main Cover

DANIELE DI NICUOLO WITH COLORS BY WALTER BAIAMONTE

Issue #14 Subscription Cover

EVAN PALMER

Issue #14 Variant Cover

KORKUT ÖZTEKIN WITH COLORS BY TRIONA FARRELL

Issue #15 Main Cover

HEATHER DANFORTH

Issue #15 Subscription Cover

PIOTR KOWALSKI WITH COLORS BY BRAD SIMPSON

Issue #15 Variant Cover

JEN BARTEL

Issue #16 Main Cover
JONATHAN LAM

Issue #16 Subscription Cover
RICHARD CHANG

Issue #16 Variant Cover
WALTER PAX
WITH COLORS BY JOANA LAFUENTE

ISCOVER
EXPLOSIVE NEW WORLDS

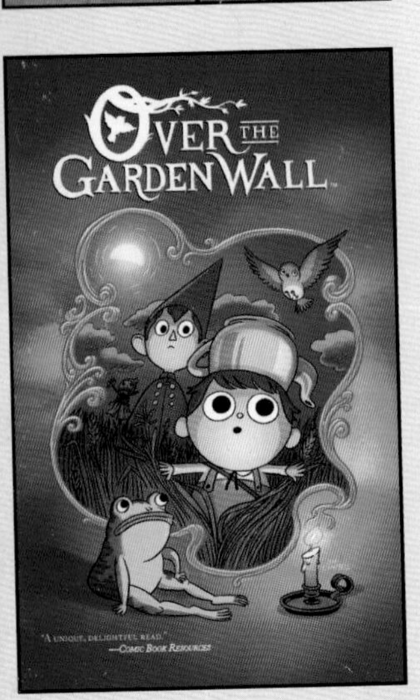

Adventure Time

...99 US

...99 US

...9 US

...4.99 US

...4.99 US

...14.99 US

Mega Princess
Kelly Thompson, Brianne Drouhard
ISBN: 978-1-68415-007-6 | $14.99 US

The Not-So Secret Society
Matthew Daley, Arlene Daley, Wook Jin Clark
ISBN: 978-1-60886-997-8 | $9.99 US

Over the Garden Wall
Patrick McHale, Jim Campbell and Others
Volume 1
ISBN: 978-1-60886-940-4 | $14.99 US
Volume 2
ISBN: 978-1-68415-006-9 | $14.99 US

Steven Universe
Rebecca Sugar and Others
Volume 1
ISBN: 978-1-60886-706-6 | $14.99 US
Volume 2
ISBN: 978-1-60886-796-7 | $14.99 US

Steven Universe & The Crystal Gems
ISBN: 978-1-60886-921-3 | $14.99 US

Steven Universe: Too Cool for School
ISBN: 978-1-60886-771-4 | $14.99 US

AVAILABLE AT YOUR LOCAL COMICS SHOP AND BOOKSTORE
To find a comics shop in your area, call 1-888-266-4226
WWW.**BOOM-STUDIOS**.COM